A BUMPER BOOK OF
CHRISTMAS
JOKES

'Mum, how long is it
until Christmas?'

'It's still a few months away,
darling. Why do you ask?'

'I was wondering if I had to
start being good yet.'

Previously published as *Christmas Jokes* in 2017 and *Christmas Cracker Jokes* in 2018

This bind-up edition published 2020 by Macmillan Children's Books
an imprint of Pan Macmillan
The Smithson, 6 Briset Street, London EC1M 5NR
EU representative: Macmillan Publishers Ireland Ltd, 1st Floor,
The Liffey Trust Centre, 117-126 Sheriff Street, Upper
Dublin 1, DO1 YC43
Associated companies throughout the world
www.panmacmillan.com

ISBN 978-1-5290-4307-5

3 5 7 9 8 6 4 2

A CIP catalogue record for this book is available from the British Library.

Compiled and illustrated by Perfect Bound Ltd
Illustrated by Dan Newman and Grace Newman
Printed and bound by CPI Group (UK) Ltd, Croydon CR0 4YY

MIX
Paper | Supporting
responsible forestry
FSC® C116313

OVER 500 JOKES

MACMILLAN CHILDREN'S BOOKS

A BUMPER BOOK OF CHRISTMAS JOKES

Contents

Christmas Crackers

Why shouldn't you eat
Christmas decorations?
You might catch tinsellitis.

Christmas is weird.
When else do you get up
early to sit indoors by a
dead tree and eat sweets
out of your sock?

What did one angel
say to the other angel?

'Halo there.'

What's green, hangs in a
doorway and croaks?

A mistle-toad.

I told Grandad that a
lot of people go to
Amazon to choose
Christmas presents.

Three days later, he rang
me from Brazil.

What's different
about the alphabet at
Christmas?
It has no 'L'.

What's the Internet's
favourite carol?
'Oh .com All Ye Faithful'.

What squeaks
and is scary?
The Ghost of
Christmouse past.

Our local bookshop
had a Christmas
sale with a third off
everything.
I bought a copy of
The Lion, the Witch.

'Why was that security
guard talking to you?'
'He told me off for trying
to do my Christmas
shopping early.'
'Why is that a problem?'
'Well, the shop wasn't
actually open.'

We like to cut down our
own Christmas tree.

**We call it Christmas
chopping.**

What do hedgehogs
eat for lunch?

Prickled onions.

What do crackers,
fruitcake and nuts
remind me of?
You!

'Doctor, I'm so excited
about Christmas that
I can't get to sleep.'
**'Well, try lying right on
the very edge of your bed.
You'll soon drop off.'**

Why do birds fly
south in the winter?
Because it's too
far to walk!

'Doctor, I'm afraid I've got a
mince pie stuck in my ear.'
'Well, I can put some
cream on it.'

What do elves write in
Christmas cards?

**Wishing you a
fairy Merry
Christmas!**

What is a parent's
favourite Christmas carol?
'Silent Night'.

What did the salt say to
the pepper on Christmas
morning?

'Seasoning's Greetings.'

How do snowmen
greet each other?
It's ice to meet you.

What did the Christmas
card say to the stamp?

**'Stick with me and we'll
go places.'**

What's the difference between Saint George and one of Father Christmas's reindeer?

One slays a dragon, the other's draggin' a sleigh.

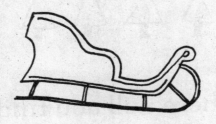

What sort of ball doesn't bounce?

A snowball.

What did the bag
of salt & vinegar
say to the bag of
cheese & onion?

'Merry Crisp-mas.'

Where will you find a
Christmas tree?

Between Christmas two
and Christmas four.

What Christmas carol gets
sung in the desert?

'O Camel Ye Faithful'.

Why can't Christmas trees knit?

Because they drop their needles.

How does Good King Wenceslas like his pizza?

Deep pan, crisp and even.

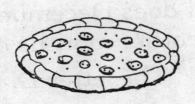

What comes at
the end of
Christmas Day?
The letter Y.

Where do ghosts go for a
treat at Christmas?

The phantomime.

What does December have
that other months don't?
The letter D.

What's the loudest part
of a Christmas tree?

The bark.

What's the difference
between a postbox and
a polar bear's bum?

**If you don't know,
I think I'll post my own
Christmas cards.**

Perfect Presents

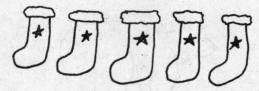

What's the first thing
you should give your
parents at Christmas?

**A list of everything
you want.**

What do snow children
have for breakfast?

Ice Krispies.

What present should you give a tiny ballerina who's too small for a tutu?

A one-one.

What's the best Christmas present?

A broken drum – you can't beat it.

My brother got a ridiculously large firework for Christmas.

He's over the moon.

I wasn't happy getting
a pocket calculator for
Christmas.
I already know how to
count my pockets.

What do you give a
hip-hop singer for
Christmas?
It doesn't matter,
as long as you wrap it.

What present do you give a
brass band who've broken all
their instruments?
A tuba glue.

Dad got a pair of trousers made from spider silk.

They look great, but the flies keep sticking.

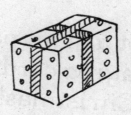

What did the farmer get for Christmas?
A cow-culator.

What's the
perfect musical
gift for a Spanish
fisherman?

Cast-a-nets.

'I got a giant pack
of playing cards for
Christmas!'

'Big deal.'

Dad got a box set
of *Doctor Who* for
Christmas.
We watched it
back to back.

Unfortunately
I wasn't the one
facing the telly.

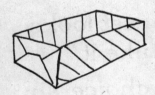

I think Father Christmas
is on a budget this year.

Mum asked for something
with diamonds in it . . .
she got a pack of cards.

'Excuse me, I'd like to get a kitten for my son.'

'Sorry, we don't do swaps.'

'No, I mean do you have any kittens going cheap?'

'Of course not, they all go miaow.'

Man: 'That train set looks brilliant, I'll take it.'

Assistant: 'Good choice, sir. I'm sure your son will love it.'

Man: 'Oh yes . . . I suppose he will. You'd better give me two then.'

'My Christmas stocking
has a hole in it!'

'Of course it does.
How else can Father
Christmas put the
presents in?'

For Christmas I wished
to have my name up in
lights all over the world.

So Mum and Dad
changed my name
to 'EXIT'.

What do witches
use to wrap
their presents?
Spell-otape.

I bought my
son a fridge for
Christmas.
I can't wait to see
his face light up
when he opens it.

Christmas Books

The Art of Kissing
    by Miss L. Toe

Winning at Charades
    by Vic Tree

Guessing your Presents
    by P. King

Bad Gifts
    by M. T. Box

How to get a Great Present
    by B. Good

Last Christmas I got a really cheap dictionary from my sister.

I couldn't find the words *to thank her.*

What do you give a dog for Christmas?

A mobile bone.

I wanted to get my dad some camouflage trousers for Christmas.

I couldn't find any.

I can't decide what to give my little brother for Christmas this year . . .

Last year I gave him chickenpox.

I dreamed Father Christmas gave me a giant marshmallow as a present.

When I woke up my pillow was missing.

For Christmas I got
a book about how they
fix ships together.

It's riveting.

'Do you have any of
those pink toy cars?'

'We've sold out, I'm afraid.
Absolutely everyone in the
whole country has bought
one this week.'

'What do you mean?'

'We've turned into a
pink car-nation.'

'Dad, can I have
a wombat for
Christmas?'

'A wombat?
What do you want
a wombat for?'

'To play wom.'

Father Christmas gave
me a huge ball of clay
this year.
I don't know what
to make of it.

I was going to give Dad
a broken pencil, but I
changed my mind.

There was no point.

I think we're going to the
cinema at Christmas to
see a film about caravans.

I've seen the trailer.

'What would you like
for Christmas? I was
thinking of getting you
a PlayStation.'

'Nothing would make
me happier!'

'OK, I'll get you
nothing then.'

We wanted some
fireworks at Christmas,
but Dad didn't light them
at the right time.

He was bang out
of order.

Father Christmas

Christmas Books

*What Do You
Do After Christmas
Dinner?*
by Clare Inup

Sledging for Beginners
by I. C. Bottom

Surprise Present!
by Omar Gosh

Father Christmas
is so strong, he can lift a
reindeer with one hand.

**The problem is, he can't
find a one-handed
reindeer to prove it.**

What's as big as
Father Christmas but
weighs nothing?

His shadow.

What did Father
Christmas call the
reindeer with two short
legs and two long legs?
Eileen.

What did he call the
reindeer with one eye
higher than the other?

Isaiah.

What did he call the
reindeer with three humps
on its back?

Humphrey.

Who delivers
Christmas presents
to pets?

Santa Paws.

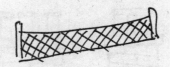

What did Father
Christmas call the
reindeer that was lying
across his tennis court?

Annette.

And what did he call
the reindeer who was
standing across a river?

Bridget.

What is a skunk's
favourite Christmas
song?

'Jingle Smells'.

What did Father
Christmas's scarf say
to his hat?

'You go on ahead,
I'll hang around here.'

Is Father Christmas
an employee?
No, he's elf-employed.

What did the spider
want for Christmas?

A new web-site.

What did Father Christmas
say to Mrs Christmas when
he looked out of the window?

'Looks like rain, dear.'

What makes Father
Christmas such a
good racing driver?

He's always in
Pole position.

Father Christmas was
inspecting the reindeer
with his wife.

'This one's legs look
a little short,' he said.

'How long do you want
them?' she replied. 'They
reach all the way to the
ground, don't they?'

How does Father Christmas get four reindeer in his sleigh?

Two on the front bench, and two on the back.

And how does he get four polar bears in his sleigh?

He takes the reindeer out.

Who is Father Christmas's favourite singer?

Elf-is Presley.

What photos does
Father Christmas take?

Elfies.

And what does he use
to take them?

His North Polaroid.

Father Christmas lost
his enormous giant
reindeer, and his tiny
baby reindeer.

**He looked high and
low for them.**

How many presents
can Father Christmas fit
in an empty sleigh?
Just one. After that,
it isn't empty.

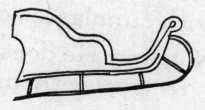

Where does Father
Christmas go swimming?
The North Pool.

What does Father
Christmas say when he
sees a herd of reindeer in
the distance?

**'Look, a herd of reindeer
in the distance.'**

What does he say when
he sees a herd of reindeer
with sunglasses on?

**Nothing. He doesn't
recognize them.**

What does he say when he sees a group of polar bears in sunglasses?

'Aha! You fooled me once with those disquises, but not this time!'

How can you tell when Father Christmas is in your house?

You can sense his presents.

Why doesn't Father Christmas go down some chimneys?
Elf and Safety regulations.

What goes 'Oh, oh, oh'?
Father Christmas walking backwards.

What can Father Christmas give to everyone and still keep?
A cold.

Why does
Father Christmas climb
down chimneys?

Because it soots him.

How can Father
Christmas tell if there's a
reindeer in his fridge?

**He looks for hoof prints
in the butter.**

If he's feeling lazy,
Father Christmas
feeds the reindeer in
his pyjamas.

**How they get in his
pyjamas is a mystery.**

What do you call
Father Christmas
when he's lying on
the beach?

Sandy Claus.

What do you call
Father Christmas
when he doesn't move?

Santa Pause.

Why does Father
Christmas buy treats for
his elf mathematicians?

**Because it's the little things
that count.**

What's red and white
and red and white
and red and white?
Father Christmas
rolling down a hill.

Father Christmas
wasn't too sure about
his beard at first.
Then it grew
on him.

Father Christmas
experimented with battery-
powered robot reindeer, but
they weren't any good.
They didn't charge
quickly enough.

What's red and white
and goes up and down,
up and down,
up and down?

**Father Christmas
on a bungee rope.**

What happened when
Father Christmas fell
asleep in a fireplace?

He slept like a log.

Father Christmas
had a couple of spare
reindeer, so he decided
to sell them on eBay
for £500.

Nobody put in a bid,
because they were
two deer.

Why is it so cold at
Christmas?

Because it's Decembrrrrr.

Why does Father
Christmas cry on
26 December?

He gets Santa-mental.

Why didn't Father
Christmas get wet when
he lost his umbrella?

It wasn't raining.

On which side of
Father Christmas's
face is his beard?

The outside.

Why does Father
Christmas worry about
getting stuck
up a chimney?

He's Claus-trophobic.

What kind of motorbike does Father Christmas ride?

A Holly-Davidson.

What is Father Christmas's wife called?

Mary Christmas.

How do you show your appreciation for Father Christmas?

Sant-applause.

Why does Father
Christmas have
three gardens?
So that he can
hoe, hoe, hoe.

Father Christmas
was just about throw
away all his socks . . .
Then he got cold feet.

What kind of coat does
Father Christmas wear if
it rains on Christmas Eve?
A wet one.

What do you call
a smelly Santa?

Farter Christmas.

What did Father
Christmas do when a
reindeer ate his pen?

He used a pencil.

Life at the North Pole

How do you get milk from a polar bear?

Wait until it's asleep, open its fridge very quietly, grab the milk, then run like mad.

Why do reindeer wear bells?

Because their horns don't work.

How do you speak to a large, angry polar bear?

From a great distance.

Why do reindeer have fur coats?

Because they'd look silly in woolly jumpers.

What's the difference
between a reindeer
and a teabag?

If you don't know
I'm not going to ask you
to make me tea.

Which reindeer has
the worst manners?

Rude-olph.

What do reindeer always
say before telling a joke?

This one will sleigh you!

What's furry, round
and smells minty?
A Polo bear.

'Keep that reindeer out of my
house! It's covered in fleas!'

'You heard, Rudolph.
Stay out of the house –
it's covered in fleas.'

What time is it
when a polar bear
sits on your igloo?

Time to get a new igloo.

What often falls at the
North Pole but never
gets hurt?

Snow.

How do you tell the
difference between a
walrus and an orange?

Try giving one a
squeeze. If you don't
get orange juice,
it's the walrus.

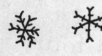

What's the difference
between a polar bear
and a banana?

You'd better find out,
because if you try to
peel a polar bear . . .

Why shouldn't you take a reindeer to the zoo?

Because they prefer the movies.

What has eight legs, four antlers and two noses?

Two reindeer!

How did Rudolph learn to read?

He was elf-taught.

How many of Father
Christmas's reindeer
can jump higher
than a pine tree?

**All of them – pine trees
can't jump.**

What do you call a
reindeer wearing earmuffs?
**Anything you like.
He can't hear you.**

What do reindeer use to
decorate their antlers?

Horn-aments.

How does Rudolph
know when Christmas
is coming?

He checks his calen-deer.

25

What's the difference
between a cookie
and a reindeer?

**Try dunking them in your
milk – then you'll know.**

Why was the reindeer
wearing black boots?
**All his brown ones
were muddy.**

Where would Rudolph
go if he lost his tail?

To a re-tail shop.

What do you call
a reindeer with
no eyes?

No idea.

What do you call a
reindeer with no eyes
and no legs?

Still no idea.

What do reindeer have
that no other animals do?

Baby reindeer.

Why was Rudolph
such a bad dancer?

**Because he had
two left feet.**

Polar bears are three metres
tall and weigh 400kg.
Where do they sleep?

Anywhere they like.

Why did the reindeer
say 'woof'?

He was learning a
foreign language.

What do snowmen
eat for breakfast?

Snowflakes.

How do you stop a
reindeer from smelling?

Put your fingers
up its nose.

Why don't reindeer
ride motorbikes?

**Their antlers won't
fit in a helmet.**

What's white, lives at
the North Pole and runs
around naked?

A polar bare.

What do you call a
reindeer with her head
stuck in a snowdrift?

**Anything you like.
She can't hear you.**

A seal will dive down
hundreds of metres
for fish . . .

Imagine what he'd do
for a portion of chips!

What do you call a
skeleton at the North Pole?

A numbskull.

What's wrong with a
reindeer with jelly in one ear
and custard in the other?

He's a trifle deaf.

What's the difference
between a blueberry
and a polar bear?

They're both blue, except
for the polar bear.

What says 'Now you see
me, now you don't, now you
see me, now you don't'?

A snowman on a
zebra crossing.

Santa's Little Helpers

Where do you
usually find elves?

Depends where
you left them.

Who holds all
Father Christmas's
books for him?
The books-elf.

What do elves use
to pay for the bells
on their hats?
Jingle bills.

What do elves make their
sandwiches from?
Shortbread.

What do Santa's
elves have for tea?
Fairy cakes.

Who is always
following the first
eleven elves?
The tw-elf.

Who runs the
North Pole Hospital?
The National Elf Service.

What did the elves
do when a polar
bear ran off with
their football?

They played tennis.

Who is the smelliest elf?
Stinkerbell.

One of the elves is so
short that when he pulls
up his socks he can't see
where he's going.

How many elves
does it take to change
a light bulb?

Ten. One to change
the bulb and nine
underneath him,
standing on each
other's shoulders.

What do elves
learn at school?
The elf-abet.

What do you call
an elf who has just
won the lottery?
Welfy.

How long is an elf's shoe?
One foot long.

What do elves play
on their days off?
Miniature golf.

What cars do elves drive?
**Either a Mini . . .
or a Toy-ota.**

Why did Father
Christmas tell off one of
his elves at dinner?

**Because he was
a-gobblin'.**

When are the elves
going to arrive?

Shortly.

Why did the elf go to
bed with a ruler?

**He wanted to see if
he slept longer.**

What time do the elves
start work?

Shortly after nine.

Why did the elf's
photos look rubbish?

**They were all
pixie-lated.**

What do elves have
for lunch?

**An hour, like
everyone else.**

Chilly Chuckles

What's an ig?

A snow house with no loo.

What does a snowmen
call his babies?

Chill-dren.

What do you call
a snowman in
summer?
A puddle.

How do I build a
shelter in the snow?
I-gloo it together.

What happened to
the snowman with
the fiery temper?

He had a meltdown.

Where do
snowmen
dance?

Snow balls.

How do you scare a
snowman?

Plug in a hairdryer.

What do you sing at a
snowman's birthday
party?
'Freeze a jolly
good fellow'.

How do snowmen
get around?
By icicle.

Where do snowmen
keep their money?

In a snow bank.

And what do they call
their money?

Iced lolly.

What do snowmen
eat for lunch?

Ice-bergers.

And what do they put
on them?

Chilly sauce.

What do snowmen
do at weekends?

Just chill out.

Why did the snowman stand on the marshmallow?
Because he didn't want to fall in the hot chocolate.

What did the snowflake say to the snowman?
Nothing. Snowflakes can't talk.

What does a bald
snowman need?

An ice cap.

How can you tell
a snowman is angry
with you?

**He gives you the
cold shoulder.**

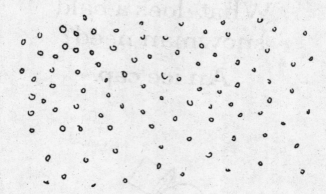

What's white and
floats upwards?
A lost snowflake.

What did the snow-
policeman say to the
snow-burglar?
'Freeze!'

What did one
snowman say to the
other snowman?
'Can you smell
carrots?'

What do Mexican
snowmen eat?
Brrr-itos . . . with
lots of chilly beans.

Eating and Drinking

What's the difference
between bogeys and
Brussels sprouts?

Kids will eat bogeys.

What's the key to a great
Christmas dinner?

A tur-key.

What two things
should you never eat
before breakfast on
Christmas Day?
Lunch and dinner.

'Mum, I think this
Christmas pudding is off.'
'Off? Where to?'

There are two
kinds of people at
Christmas.

People who eat too
much chocolate,
and liars.

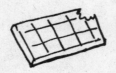

Who's never hungry
at Christmas?

The turkey, because
it's always stuffed.

What do you get if
you cross a turkey
with an octopus?

**Enough drumsticks
for everybody.**

Last year's turkey really
tickled the palate.

**Mum forgot to take
the feathers off.**

What do you call someone who's eaten a whole Christmas turkey?

An ambulance.

Mum: 'You've been no help this Christmas.'

Dad: 'What do you mean? I bought the turkey, and plucked it, and stuffed it. Now all you've got to do is kill it and put it in the oven.'

Last Christmas Mum's
gravy was very thick.
**When she stirred it, the
room went round.**

'I'm worried that the
Christmas cake I gave
you was a bit hard.'

**'Oh, don't worry –
it was perfect.'**

'Really?'

**'Yes, a slice was just right
to fix our wobbly table.'**

Who beats his chest,
swings from
Christmas cake to
Christmas cake and
smells of almonds?

Tarzipan.

Why did the Christmas
cake go to the doctor?

Because he felt crummy.

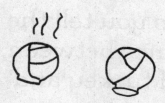

Mum: 'Eat your Brussels sprouts – they're good for growing children.'

Son: 'Why would I want to grow children?'

What do zombies put on their Christmas dinner?

Grave-y.

How do you tell the
difference between
tinned turkey and
tinned ham?

Read the labels.

What food should you
never trust at Christmas?

Mince spies.

Why is a Christmas cake
like the sea?

**Because it's full of
currants.**

What do
redcurrants say
to each other at
Christmas?

"Tis the season
to be jelly!'

How do you find out
if a turkey is stupid
and foolish?

Ask if it's looking
forward to
Christmas.

Knock, Knock - Christmas!

Knock, knock!
Who's there?
Gladys.
Gladys who?
Gladys nearly Christmas!

Knock, knock!
Who's there?
Hannah.
Hannah who?
Hannah partridge in a pear tree.

Knock, knock!
Who's there?
Arthur.
Arthur who?
Arthur any more
mince pies?

Knock, knock!
Who's there?
Our Wayne.
Our Wayne who?
Our Wayne in a manger,
no crib for a bed . . .

Knock, knock!
Who's there?
Holly.
Holly who?
Holly-days are
here again.

Knock, knock!
Who's there?
Doughnut.
Doughnut who?
Doughnut open until
Christmas!

Knock, knock!
Who's there?
Police.
Police who?
Police don't make
me eat Brussels
sprouts again.

Knock, knock!
Who's there?
Mary and Abby.
Mary and Abby who?
Mary Christmas and
Abby New Year!

Knock, knock!
Who's there?
Wanda!
Wanda who?
Wanda know what
you're getting for
Christmas?

Knock, knock!
Who's there?
Rabbit.
Rabbit who?
Rabbit carefully – it's a
Christmas present.

Knock, knock!
Who's there?
Irish.
Irish who?
Irish you a Merry
Christmas!

Knock, knock!
Who's there?
Snow.
Snow who?
Snow use – I've
forgotten my name again!

Knock, knock!
Who's there?
Wenceslas.
Wenceslas who?
Wenceslas train home?

Knock, knock!
Who's there?
Oakham.
Oakham who?
Oakham all ye faithful . . .

Knock, knock!
Who's there?
Avery.
Avery who?
Avery Merry Christmas!

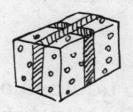

Knock, knock!
Who's there?
Elf.
Elf who?
Elf me wrap this
present for Santa!

Festive Animals

What do you call a chicken
at the North Pole?

Lost.

Who brings presents to all
the little furry creatures?
Father Christmouse.

What sort of
insects love snow?
Mo-ski-toes.

**Which bird
should you ask
to write your
Christmas cards?**
**A ballpoint
pen-quin.**

Who brings presents to
all the little sharks?

Santa Jaws.

Why did the turkey
join a band?

**Because it already had
the drumsticks.**

What do you get if
you cross a snowman
with a shark?

Frostbite.

What do sheep say
to each other on
Christmas morning?

**'Merry Christmas to
ewe . . . and season's
bleatings.'**

What do angry rodents
send each other in
December?

Cross-mouse cards.

Why wouldn't the baby lobster share her Christmas presents?

Because she's a little shellfish.

How do you get four walruses in a Mini?

Two in the front, two in the back.

How do you get four Father Christmases in a Mini?

Don't be silly, there's only one Father Christmas.

How do you know there
are two walruses in
your fridge?

**You hear giggling when
the light goes out.**

How do you know there
are three walruses in
your fridge?

You can't close the door.

How do you know there
are four walruses in
your fridge?
There's an empty Mini
parked outside.

What's a dog's
favourite carol?
'Bark! The Herald
Angels Sing'.

What do you get if you
cross Father Christmas
with a duck?

A Christmas quacker.

Why don't
polar bears
eat penguins?
**They can't get the
wrappers off.**

One Christmas, It Was So Cold...

... we would empty the freezer and huddle round it to get warm.

... words would freeze as you spoke them. You had to grab them out of the air and thaw them out by the fire to find out what someone had said!

... dogs would be stuck
to lamp posts.

... I needed a hammer
and chisel to get my
coat off.

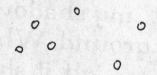

... when farmers
milked their cows,
they got ice cream.

One Christmas, it was so cold...

...I chipped a tooth
on my soup.

...when I turned on the
shower, it hailed.

...when I tried to open my
post, the letter snapped.

...my shadow stuck to the
ground. When I walked
off, it shattered.

...the fog froze
and I had to dig a
tunnel to school.

... barbers cut hair with an axe. If the hair was really long, they got out a chainsaw.

... Dad started using chilli sauce as aftershave so that he could feel his face.

... I had to break the smoke off my chimney.

... when Dad tried to take the rubbish out, it refused to go.

... wee-cicles. (You know what I'm talking about.)

Cracker Classics

What do trees do
on the internet?

They log on.

Who built the
Round Table for
King Arthur?

Sir Cumference.

What did one traffic
light say to the other?
'Don't look! I'm
changing.'

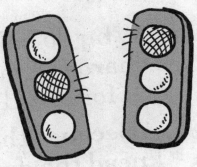

What does the sea say
to the beach?
Nothing – it just waves.

Why can't bicycles stand up on their own?

Because they're two-tyred.

Why do bakers charge so much for bread?

Because they knead the dough.

Thanks for explaining the word 'many' to me . . .

. . . it means a lot.

I went to the zoo. They
had a baguette in a cage.
It was bread in captivity.

How does a gardener fix
a hole in his jeans?

With a vegetable patch.

What kind of
flowers grow on
your face?

Two-lips.

Where should you
take a sick flower?

Hospetal.

Why did my dad get fired
from the banana factory?

He kept chucking out
the bent ones.

Last night I prepared
a candlelit dinner.

It was terrible – barely
cooked and all smoky.

What are invisible
and smell of
bananas?

Monkey burps.

What should you do if
you see a spaceman?

Park in it, man.

I stayed up all night,
wondering where
the sun had gone.
**Eventually, it
dawned on me.**

I went window-shopping
at the weekend.

I bought thirty windows.

I regret buying that
ice-cream van.

It melted.

Why did the Jelly
Baby go to school?

**Because he wanted
to be a Smartie.**

What's the difference
between a bus driver
and a cold?

**One knows the stops,
and the other stops
the nose.**

Why did the child eat
a pound coin?

Because his mum said it
was his dinner money.

My cousin is named
after his father.
He's called 'Dad'.

What's the hardest part
of making chocolate
chip cookies?

Peeling all the Smarties.

How do you make
antifreeze?

Hide her woolly jumper.

Did you hear
about the cowboy
who wore paper
boots, paper jeans,
a paper shirt and
a paper hat?

**He was arrested
for rustling.**

Thieves have stolen two baths and a shower.
They made a clean getaway.

What do burglars have at bedtime?
Milk and crookies.

I slept like a baby last night.
I woke up crying every two hours.

I went to the gym
to learn how to
weightlift.

I'm beginning to
pick it up.

For some reason, I can
only remember
twenty-five letters
of the alphabet.

I don't know Y.

I put a whiteboard
and rows of desks
in my bedroom.
It looks really classy.

Yesterday I fell
down a deep
dark hole.

**I didn't see
that well.**

Whenever I ride my
bike, I ride it twice.

**I'm very keen on
recycling.**

I told my mum
she'd drawn
her eyebrows
on too high.
She looked
pretty surprised.

I wanted to make a
ballet skirt, but I didn't
know where to start.
Then I put tu
and tu together.

What do hippies do?
They hold
your leggies on.

What's green and furry, has six legs and can't swim?

A pool table.

My granny's very tall and thin, with a big round head.

She's a lollipop lady.

What's round,
bright and silly?
A fool moon.

What do you call
a lost meteorite?
A meteowrong.

Where does a general
keep his armies?
Up his sleevies.

Food Funnies

What did the fast-walking tomato say to the slow-walking tomato?

Ketchup!

What do you give to a sick lemon?

Lemonaid.

What's miserable and
covered in custard?

Apple grumble.

What is square
and yellow?

**A lemon in
disguise.**

What do you call
fake spaghetti?

An impasta.

Which cheese do you use
to encourage a bear?

Camembert.

Which cheese is
not yours?

Nacho cheese.

What kind of cheese is
made backwards?

Edam.

What does cheese
say when it looks
in the mirror?

Halloumi.

Which cheese do
you use to disguise
a small horse?

Mascarpone.

How do you handle
dangerous cheese?

Caerphilly.

What colour is a burp?
Burple.

Why did the jelly wobble?
It saw the milkshake.

What's the fastest vegetable?
A runner bean.

What's green and goes 'boing, boing'?

A spring onion.

What vegetable is always wet?

A leek.

Why did the orange take the day off school?

It wasn't peeling well.

Name two things
you can't eat for
breakfast.

Lunch and dinner.

What's small, red
and whispers?

A hoarse radish.

What
happened
to the grape
when it was
stepped on?

**It let out a little
whine.**

What's a dog's
favourite pizza?

Pupperoni.

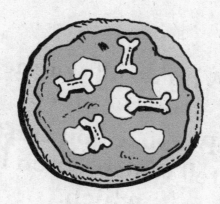

Where do tough
chickens come from?

Hard-boiled eggs.

Frightful Funnies

Why do all witches look the same?

Because you can't tell which witch is which.

How do
you make a
witch itch?

Take away
the 'w'.

What do
witches
use to stay
pale in the
summer?

Suntan
potion.

Why are ghosts so
bad at lying?

You can see right
through them.

How do ghosts
like their eggs?

Terrorfried.

What do ghosts
eat for dinner?

Spookhetti.

And what do ghosts
eat for pudding?

I scream.

Where do phantoms
buy stamps?

At the ghost office.

Why didn't the
skeleton
go to the party?
**He had no body
to go with.**

How do
skeletons
catch up with
friends?
**By mobile
bone.**

How can you tell there's a
baby skeleton nearby?
You can hear its rattle.

Do all zombies
have girlfriends?
Only the good-
lurking ones.

On what day do
monsters eat people?
Chewsday.

What do you say
to a monster with
three heads?
'Hello, hello, hello!'

What do you do if a
monster knocks
on your door?

Don't answer it.

Where does a monster
sit on the train?

Anywhere she likes!

What's a sea monster's
favourite meal?

Fish and ships.

What's hairy, scary and
goes up and down?

**A monster on a
trampoline.**

What do you give a
seasick monster?

Plenty of room.

Which monster
loves dancing?
The boogieman.

Who is the
cleverest monster?
Frank Einstein.

How do ghosts go
on holiday?
By scaroplane.

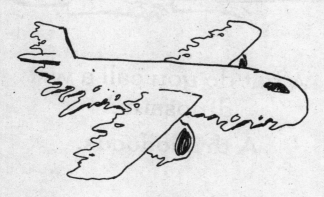

Dippy Dinosaurs

What do you call a
sleeping dinosaur?

A stegosnorus.

What do you call a wet
dinosaur?

A driplodocus.

What do you call a
destructive dinosaur?
Tyrannosaurus
wrecks.

What makes more noise
than a hungry dinosaur?
Two hungry dinosaurs.

What do triceratops sit on?
Tricerabottoms.

Which dinosaurs
could jump higher
than a house?

All of them –
houses can't jump.

What do you call a
T-rex with a banana
in each ear?

Anything you like –
it can't hear you.

Which was the
scariest dinosaur?
The terrordactyl.

What did dinosaurs
have that no other
creature has?

Baby dinosaurs.

Do you know how long
dinosaurs roamed the earth?

Exactly the same way as
short dinosaurs.

What dinosaur
never gives up?

The try-try-tryceratops.

What do you call a
one-eyed dinosaur?

Doyouthinkhesaurus.

What do you call a one-
eyed dinosaur's dog?

Doyouthinkhesaurus rex.

Why do they have
old dinosaur bones
in the museum?

They can't afford
new ones.

What do you get when
a T-rex sneezes?

Out of the way.

Knock, Knock!

Knock, knock!
Who's there?
Interrupting cow.
Interrup–

MOOOO!

Knock, knock!
Who's there?
Europe.
Europe who?
No I'm not!

Knock, knock!
Who's there?
Hatch.
Hatch who?
Bless you!

Knock, knock!
Who's there?
Lettuce.
Lettuce who?
Lettuce in please!

Knock, knock!
Who's there?
Cows go.
Cows go who?
No, they go 'moo', silly!

Knock, knock!
Who's there?
Boo.
Boo who?
Don't cry,
it's only a joke!

Knock, knock!
Who's there?
Eye nose.
Eye nose
who?
Eye nose
loads of
jokes like
this!

Knock, knock!
Who's there?
Ivor Dunnup.
Ivor Dunnup who?
I wondered what the
smell was!

Knock, knock!
Who's there?
Wooden shoe.
Wooden shoe who?
Wooden shoe like to hear
another joke?

Knock, knock!
Who's there?
Tank.
Tank who?
You're welcome.

Knock, knock!
Who's there?
Avenue.
Avenue who?
Avenue realized it's
me yet?

Knock, knock!
Who's there?
Eva.
Eva who?
Eva you let me in
or I call the police.

Knock, knock!
Who's there?
Police.
Police who?
Police will you let me in!

Doctor, Doctor!

Doctor, doctor,
I'm frightened of
two-letter words!

Really?

Yes, I can't even
think about it.

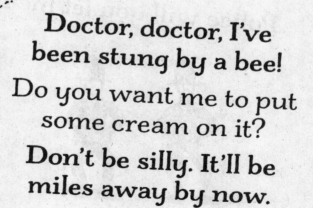

Doctor, doctor, I've
been stung by a bee!

Do you want me to put
some cream on it?

Don't be silly. It'll be
miles away by now.

Doctor, doctor,
I think I'm a dustbin!
Oh, you're full
of rubbish.

Doctor, doctor,
everyone ignores me.
Next patient, please!

Doctor, doctor, I'm losing
my memory.
I see. When did this start?
When did what start?

Doctor, doctor, I think
I'm a pair of curtains!
**You need to pull
yourself together.**

Doctor, doctor, I've just
been beaten up by an
enormous insect!
**I think there's a
nasty bug going round.**

Doctor, doctor, I've got a
sausage up my nose and
mash in my ears!

**I don't think you've been
eating properly.**

Doctor, doctor, I've hurt
my arm in two places!

**Well don't go back
to those places again.**

What Do You Get . . .

What do you get if you cross a sheep with a kangaroo?

A woolly jumper.

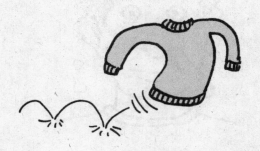

What do you get if you cross a parrot with a centipede?

A walkie-talkie.

What do you get if
you cross a kangaroo
with an elephant?

**Massive holes all
over Australia.**

What do you get if you
cross a blue cat with
a red parrot?

A purple carrot.

What do you get if
you cross a snake with
a hedgehog?
Barbed wire.

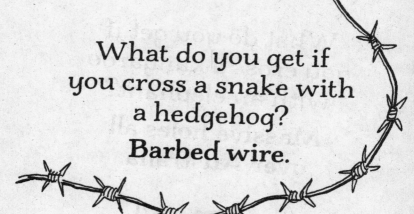

What do you get if
you cross a pudding
with a cowpat?

A smelly jelly.

What do you
get if you cross
a chicken with a
cement mixer?

A brick layer.

What do you get
if you cross ten
cars with some
strawberries?

A traffic jam.

What do you get if you
cross a cheetah with
a hamburger?
Really fast food.

What do you get
if you cross an
elephant with a fish?
Swimming trunks.

What do you get if
you cross a cuddly
toy with a fridge?

A teddy brrrrr.

What do you get if
you cross a cocker
spaniel, a poodle
and a rooster?

A cockerpoodledoo.

Fairy Tales

Who shouted
'Bum!' at the Big
Bad Wolf?

Little Rude Riding
Hood.

What pet did
Aladdin have?

A flying carpet.

Who flies through the
air in his underwear?
Peter Pants.

Why do dragons
sleep all day?
**So they can fight
knights.**

How does Captain Hook
wake up in the morning?
He has an alarm croc.

Why is Cinderella so bad at football?

She keeps running away from the ball.

Why would Snow White make a good judge?

Because she is the fairest of them all.

Who is the funniest
princess?
RaPUNzel.

Which fairy is
the smelliest?
Stinkerbell.

Who is beautiful,
grey and wears
glass slippers?
Cinderelephant.

Creepy-crawlies

What do you call
an evil insect?
A baddy-long-legs.

MWAH HAH HAAH

What did the
grumpy bee say?
'Buzz off!'

What's black and
yellow and goes
'zzub, zzub'?

A bee flying backwards.

What is the largest
kind of ant?

A giant.

Where do you take
a sick insect?

To the waspital.

Why couldn't the
centipede be in the
football team?

Because she took too
long to put her boots on.

Why did the
fly fly?
Because the
spider spied 'er.

What's the
difference between
a fly and a bird?
A bird can fly, but a
fly can't bird.

What do bees like to chew?
Bumblegum.

Why do bees hum?
Because they've
forgotten the words.

What do you
call an ant with
ten eyes?
Ant-ten-eye.

What do you call a fly
with no wings?
A walk.

What's worse that
finding a slug in
your sandwich?

Finding half a slug.

How can you tell which
end of a worm is which?

**Tickle the middle and see
which end laughs.**

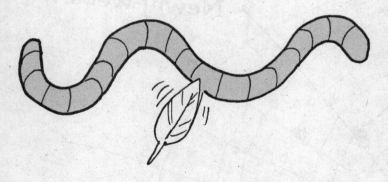

Where can you
find giant snails?

**At the end of
giants' fingers.**

What do you call two
spiders that have just
got married?

Newly-webs.

What are caterpillars
afraid of?

Dogerpillars.

How do fleas get
from dog to dog?

They itch-hike.

Sea Sillies

Which fish goes well
with ice cream?

A jellyfish.

Which fish is the
most valuable?

A goldfish.

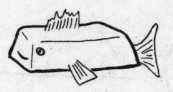

What is a knight's
favourite fish?

A swordfish.

What's the best
way to get in
touch with
a fish?

Drop it a line.

Why do lobsters
not like sharing?

Because they're
shellfish.

How do little squids
go to school?

By octobus.

What do you
call a fish with
three eyes?

Fiiish.

How do you cut an ocean?
With a sea-saw.

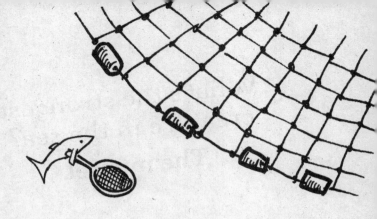

Why are fish no
good at tennis?

They don't like to get
too close to the net.

Why did the
lobster blush?

Because the seaweed!

What's the strongest
creature in the sea?
The mussel.

What do sea
creatures watch
in the evening?
Telefishion.

What happened to
the cold jellyfish?
It set.

What do baby
sharks get before
they go to sleep?
A bite-time story.

How do sea creatures
carry big things?
In a whalebarrow.

What does an oyster
do on her birthday?

She shellebrates.

Why do dolphins
swim in salt water?

**Because pepper
makes them sneeze.**

CHOO!

What should you do
with creased seals?

Use a seal-iron.

I've got two octopuses that look exactly alike.

I think they may be itentacle.

Why is it easy to weigh fish?

They come with their own scales.

Pirate Puns

Why did the
pirate cross
the sea?

To get to the
other tide.

What has eight eyes
and eight legs?

Eight pirates.

Where do pirates buy Christmas presents?

Arrrrrrrgos.

How can you tell if you're a pirate?

If you arrr, you are.

How much do pirates
pay for ear piercings?
A buck-an-ear.

When does a
pirate stand at
the very back end
of his ship?
When he's being stern.

Where do pirates
go to the toilet?

On the poop deck.

How do pirates get
from ship to ship?

By taxi crab.

Why couldn't the
pirates play cards?

**Because the captain was
standing on the deck.**

What do you call
a pirate who is
missing an eye?
Prate.

Why don't pirates
get hungry on
desert islands?

Because of all the sand
which is there.

Where does a pirate
keep his treasure chest?

Inside his treasure shirt.

Is it expensive to
join a pirate crew?

**Yes – it'll cost you
an arm and a leg.**

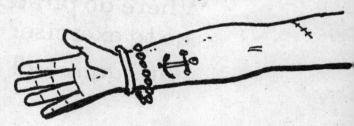

What lies shivering at the
bottom of the sea?

A nervous wreck.

Why is it really hard
to give up being a
pirate?

You get hooked.

Where do pirates
go to exercise?

Our gym, lad!

How do you spot a fuel-
efficient pirate ship?

**It does sixty miles to
the galleon.**

What do you call a
pirate with two legs
and two eyes?

A trainee.

Animal Crackers

What do you call a
donkey with three legs?

A wonkey.

What do you call a
three-legged donkey
with one eye?

A winky wonkey.

Why should you
never play games
in the jungle?

Because there are
too many cheetahs.

How do you stop a
skunk smelling?

Hold its nose.

What do you get if
you sit under a cow?
A pat on the head.

What's a cow's
favourite party game?
Moosical chairs.

What kind of pet
makes the most noise?
A trumpet.

What do you call a
cow eating grass?
A lawnmooer.

How do cows
cheat in tests?
**They copy off
each udder.**

How do you make
instant elephant?

Open the packet, add
water – and run.

What do you give a
sick elephant?

A get-wellephant card.

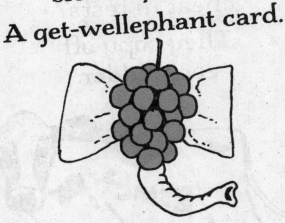

Why are elephants large,
wrinkled and grey?

Because if they were
small, smooth and green,
they'd be grapes.

What's big, grey and
doesn't matter?

An irrelephant.

Why are elephants
so wrinkled?
**Well, have you ever
tried ironing one?**

What's big,
grey and invisible?

No elephants.

What do you call a cat
with eight legs?

An octopuss.

What does a cat
put in its drink?

Mice cubes.

What do cats eat
for breakfast?

Mice Krispies.

What kinds of stories
do cats like?

Furry tales.

Did you hear about the
cat that swallowed a
ball of wool?

She had mittens.

What's the opposite
of a flabby tabby?

An itty-bitty kitty.

Why did the dog
smell of onions?

It was a hot dog.

Why don't dogs
drive cars?

**They can never find
a barking space.**

What did the dog
say to the bone?

**'It's been nice
gnawing you.'**

How do you stop a
dog barking in the
front garden?

Put it in the back
garden.

Why does my dog
keep scratching
herself?

Because she's the only
one who knows where
she itches.

Why don't dogs
watch DVDs?

They can only
press 'Paws'.

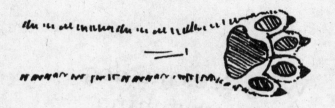

Why can't Dalmatians
play hide-and-seek?
They're always spotted.

What do rabbits sing
at birthday parties?
'Hoppy birthday to you ...'

What do you call a
rabbit with fleas?

Bugs Bunny.

Why did the rabbit
cross the road?

It was the chicken's day off.

Where can you find a
tortoise with no legs?

**Exactly where
you left it.**

What pet is
always smiling?

A grinny pig.

What's a mouse's
favourite game?

Hide-and-squeak.

What goes
'hiss, swish,
hiss, swish'?

**A windscreen
viper.**

What is a snake's
favourite school
subject?

Hisstory.

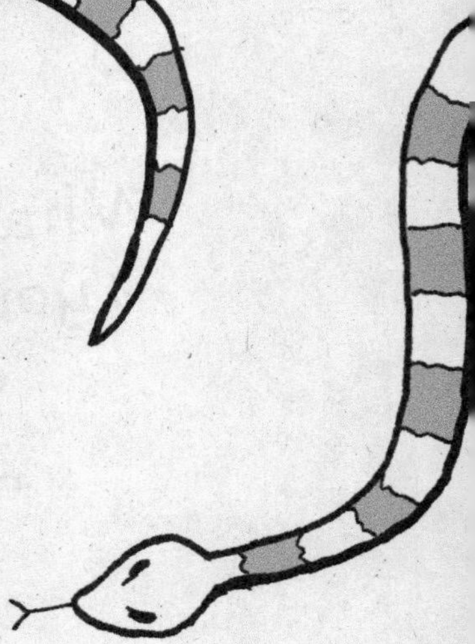

What swings through
the trees and tastes
good with milk?

**A chocolate chimp
cookie.**

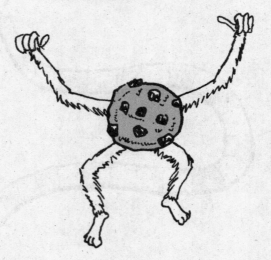

What kind of key do
you use to open
a banana?

A monkey.

Why do monkeys
have big nostrils?

Because they've got
big fingers.

Where do baby
apes sleep?

In apricots.

How do chimpanzees
make toast?

They put a slice of bread
under a gorilla.

Can chimpanzees fly?
No, but hot air
baboons can.

How do you fix a
broken chimpanzee?

With a monkey
wrench.

What do you call an
exploding monkey?
A ba-boom!

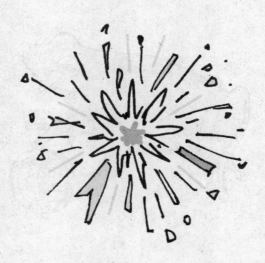

What do you give a
grumpy gorilla for its
birthday?

**I'm not sure, but you'd
better hope he likes it.**

Where do frogs keep
their money?

In a river bank.

What do you get if
you cross a frog with
a fizzy drink?

Croaka-Cola.

What does a frog eat
with a burger?
French flies.

What do frogs eat
for breakfast?
Coco Hops.

What is a frog's
favourite flower?
A croakus.

What happens
when a duck flies
upside down?
It quacks up.

Why are birds
so great?
**Because they always
suck seed.**

Where do birds
go to eat?

A nestaurant.

What do you call
a woodpecker
with no beak?

A headbanger.

What do birds say at
Halloween?
Trick or tweet?

What do you call a chicken
staring at a lettuce?

Chicken sees a salad.

'Why have you bought
all those birds?'

**'They were going
cheep.'**

How do you find out
the price of a sheep?
Just scan its baa-code.

Where do sheep go to
get their fleece cut?
The baa-baas.

What do you give
a sick bird?
Tweetment.

What do you call
bears with no ears?

B.

My pony only wants
to be ridden after dark,
which is really annoying.

She's a total night mare.

How do you move a
really heavy pig?

**With a pork-lift
truck.**

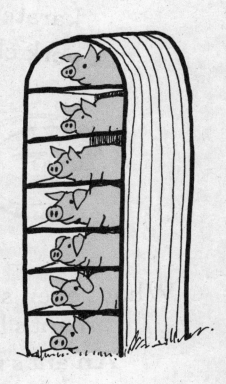

How do
you fit lots
of pigs on a
small farm?

**Build a
styscraper.**

How does a pig
get to hospital?
In a hambulance.

What do you call
a pig that does
karate?
A pork chop.

What's even smaller than
an ant's lunch?
An ant's mouth.

What's black and white and will have you in stitches?

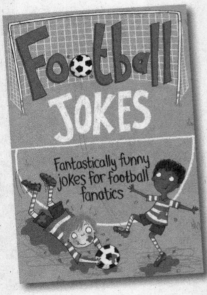

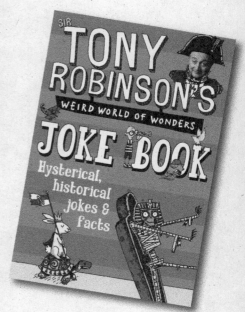